Lumpito
AND THE
PAINTER FROM SPAIN

Story by MONICA KULLING

Art by DEAN GRIFFITHS

pajamapress

Acknowledgements

This story drew its inspiration from David Douglas Duncan's *Picasso & Lump: A Dachshund's Odyssey*, published by Bulfinch Press, 2006.

My thanks to Nancy Ennis, who reads every version of every story with patience and kind wisdom; to Gail Winskill for "seeing" the story in pictures and choosing a brilliant illustrator; and to Ann Featherstone for her stellar editing skills. –M.K.

Thanks to my "moms," Gail and Ann; Rebecca for her genius; Monica for such a wonderful story; my friends at Copy Cat; my actual mom and family for so much; and my beautiful, tiny Holly, who loves books as much as I do. –D.G.

First published in the United States in 2013
Text copyright © Monica Kulling
Illustration copyright © Dean Griffiths
This edition copyright © 2012 Pajama Press

10 9 8 7 6 5 4 3 2 1

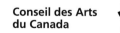

Canada Council for the Arts   **Conseil des Arts du Canada**

ONTARIO ARTS COUNCIL CONSEIL DES ARTS DE L'ONTARIO

The publisher gratefully acknowledges the support of the Canada Council for the Arts and the Ontario Arts Council for its publishing program. We acknowledge the financial support of the Government of Canada through the Canada Book Fund (CBF) for our publishing activities.

Library and Archives Canada Cataloguing in Publication

Kulling, Monica, 1952-

    Lumpito and the painter from Spain / Monica

Kulling ; illustrated by Dean Griffiths.

ISBN 978-1-927485-00-2

    1. Picasso, Pablo, 1881-1973--Juvenile fiction.

2. Dachshunds--Juvenile fiction. I. Griffiths, Dean, 1967-

II. Title.

PS8571.U54L86 2012   jC813'.54   C2012-903349-9

Publisher Cataloging-in-Publication Data (U.S.)

Kulling, Monica, 1952- .

    Lumpito and the painter from Spain / Monica Kulling ;   illustrated by Dean Griffiths.
[ ] p. : col. ill. ;   cm.
Summary: Lump the dachshund is excited to escape his housemate, Big Dog the bully, and to visit a painter in southern France. There Lump and Pablo Picasso become fast friends, and the little dog finds a new name and a new home.
ISBN-13: 978-1-927485-00-2
1. Picasso, Pablo, 1881-1973 – Juvenile fiction.   2. Dachshunds – Juvenile fiction. I. Griffiths, Dean, 1967- . II. Title.
[E] dc23   PZ7.K8665Lu   2012

Manufactured by Sheck Wah Tong Printing Ltd.
Printed in Hong Kong, China.

Pajama Press Inc.
469 Richmond St E, Toronto Ontario, Canada
www.pajamapress.ca

Distributed in the U.S. by **Orca Book Publishers**
PO Box 468 Custer, WA, 98240-0468, USA

Years ago there lived a dachshund named Lump.
His name was pronounced Loomp, which means *rascal* in German.

Lump lived in Rome with Big Dog and a photographer named David.

Lump and Big Dog were NOT best friends.
At mealtimes, Lump ate quickly so that Big Dog could not gobble up his food.
At bedtime, Lump slept with one eye open because he was afraid of what
Big Dog might do.

Even playtime was not fun for Lump. Big Dog rolled him around,
just like a football!

One day Lump woke up to wonderful news.
"Come, Lump!" called David. "We're off to meet a famous painter."

David packed his car with cameras and film.
There was only room for one small dog.
Lump chased his tail in excitement.
Goodbye, Big Dog!

The car doors opened like a gull in flight.
Lump hopped in and the travelers took off.

They flew to the south of France on winding, hilly roads.
Lump's ears flapped in the breeze. He was as happy as a lark.

At the beautiful villa a man
burst out of the doors to greet them.
He was Pablo Picasso.
"*Buenos dias, amigo!*" he called. "Welcome!"

Lump caught the painter's gaze.
His eyes were dark as a desert night,
fierce as a bull's, and warm like the Spanish sun.

The villa's doors flew open again and out bolted … a Big Dog!
Lump stood his ground. He was NOT going to let another big dog
push him around.

The dog, whose name was Yan, lay on his back.
He wanted to be friends.

The two dogs ran into the garden to play in the tangled grass.
Lump sniffed one of the stone goats. Surprise!
The goat sniffed back and gave him a friendly nudge.

"Lumpito has met Esmeralda!" roared the painter.
Lump liked the sound of his new name.
Lumpito. It had a happy ring to it.

The painter's wife, Jacqueline, called out, "*La Comida!* Lunch!"
The smell of fish filled Lumpito's nostrils.
His tummy growled. He was so excited he could hardly breathe.
Food! And there was no Big Dog to steal one bit of it.

Lumpito ate and ate. He picked the bones clean.
So did Picasso.

Picasso lay on the ground beside Lumpito.
"Things look different from down here,"
he said, stroking Lumpito's long body.

"Such a beautiful shape," said the painter dreamily.
If Lumpito had been a cat, he would have purred.

At supper, Picasso gave Lumpito a special gift—
a plate with a drawing on it.

Lumpito sniffed the plate, but it didn't smell special.
Even so, Picasso's joy made the little dog wag his long dog tail.

Night wrapped the villa in stars. Everyone slept.
Lumpito and Picasso did not.

They stood looking at the moon, listening
for the night to share its secrets.

In the morning, Lumpito saw a white rabbit in the room.
It didn't smell like a rabbit, but Lumpito raced toward it and grabbed its ears.
It didn't feel like a rabbit, but Lumpito shook it and chewed.

He tore the rabbit to shreds!
Picasso roared with laughter. "Lumpito loves my paper rabbit!

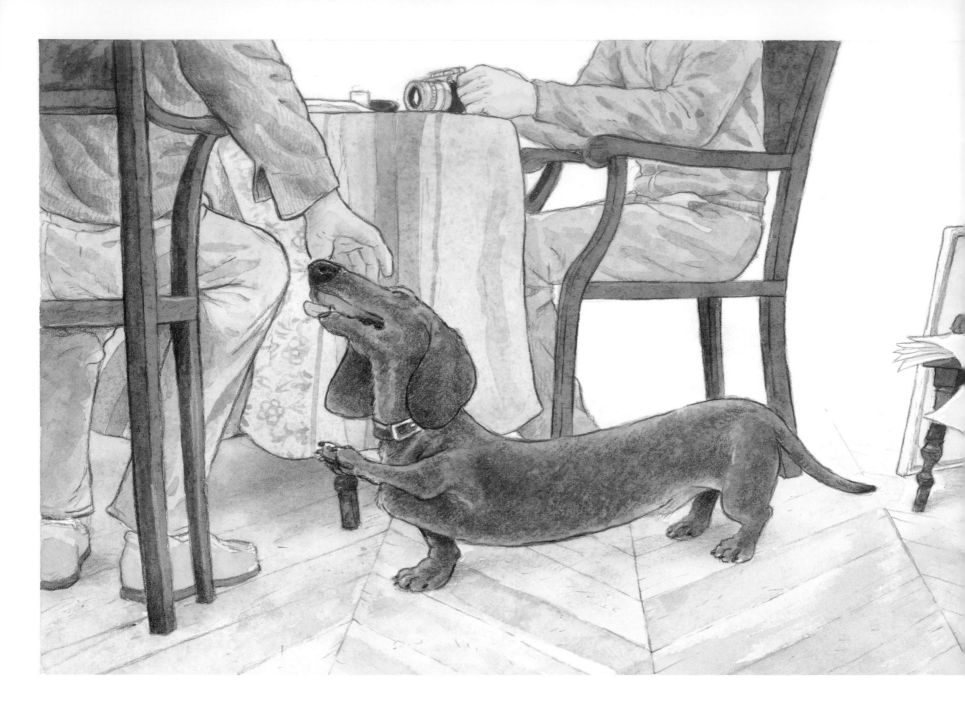

Lumpito smelled meat on the breakfast table
and waited patiently beside Picasso's chair.
"I think Lumpito has found a new home," said David.
"Rome is not a happy place for him. I travel too much,
and Big Dog is not Lumpito's friend."

Picasso picked Lumpito up and the long dog ate from his plate.
"Lumpito will stay with me," agreed Picasso.

Lumpito was happy. He ate all his meals with Picasso.

He curled on the floor next to Esmeralda and slept with both eyes closed.
And playtime with Yan was always fun.

Lumpito did not only inspire drawings; he also found his way into several paintings. Picasso's large painting called *Las Meninas* or *The Maids of Honor* was based on an old Spanish painting. The original has a big dog in it. In Picasso's version, you will find a funny black dog with perky ears. That's Lump!